SPIDER-MAN

SPIDE

THWIP!

Writer: **Paul Tobin**
Pencilers: **Matteo Lolli & Jacopo Camagni**
Inkers: **Christian Vecchia & Jacopo Camagni**
Colors: **Guru eFX & Sotocolor**
Letters: **Dave Sharpe**
Cover Artist: **Skottie Young**
Assistant Editor: **Michael Horwitz**
Editor: **Nathan Cosby**

Collection Editor: **Cory Levine**
Assistant Editors: **Alex Starbuck & John Denning**
Editors, Special Projects: **Jennifer Grünwald & Mark D. Beazley**
Senior Editor, Special Projects: **Jeff Youngquist**
Senior Vice President of Sales: **David Gabriel**
Vice President of Creative: **Tom Marvelli**

Editor in Chief: **Joe Quesada**
Publisher: **Dan Buckley**
Executive Producer: **Alan Fine**

#53

MIDTOWN HIGH SCHOOL. QUEENS, NEW YORK.
MONDAY: 12:36 P.M.
SHE'S NERVOUS ABOUT TRANSFERRING HERE. EXCITED, TOO.
AND, I'M READING SOME WORRY OVER HER DAD BEING A POLICE OFFICER.
HE'S WORRIED ABOUT GETTING CUT FROM THE BASKETBALL TEAM. AND HE'S WORRIED THAT HIS BEST FRIEND WILL FIND OUT HE'S DATING HIS SISTER.
SERIOUSLY? HOW LONG CAN HE HIDE SOMETHING LIKE THAT?
PEOPLE ALWAYS THINK THEY CAN HIDE THINGS.
WANTS TO BE FRIENDS.
WANTS TO BE MORE THAN FRIENDS.
EMMA, I FEEL KINDA BAD ABOUT DOING THIS.
YOU'RE NOT DOING ANYTHING EXCEPT LISTENING, AND I'M OKAY WITH USING MY POWERS TO PEEK INTO OTHER PEOPLE'S MINDS, SO... NO PROBLEM.
AHH, HERE WE GO.
WANTS MONEY.
WANTS MONEY.
WANTS MONEY.
WANTS MONEY.

WE WANT ALL THE PAYROLL GOLD!!
MIDTOWN HIGH, THIS IS A HOLDUP!
NOW THIS SHOULD BE VERY INTERESTING.
KEEP AN EYE ON PETER PARKER.
PAYROLL GOLD?
Le Sauce Olympus
BY PAUL TOBIN AND MATTEO LOLLI
INKS CHRISTIAN VECCHIA
COLORS GURU eFX LETTERS DAVE SHARPE
COVER SKOTTIE YOUNG
PRODUCTION DAMIEN LUCCHESE
EDITOR NATHAN COSBY
EDITOR IN CHIEF JOE QUESADA
PUBLISHER DAN BUCKLEY
EXEC. PRODUCER ALAN FINE
A SENSE OF RESPONSIBILITY

WHAT'S PETER THINKING?
I'M READING CONFUSION.
HE HAS SOME SORT OF SPECIAL SENSE THAT WARNS HIM ABOUT DANGER, BUT HE'S GETTING MIXED SIGNALS.
HE'S WONDERING IF THERE'S SOMETHING ELSE, APART FROM THESE GUYS.
OH. OH THAT'S...IT'S US, ISN'T IT?
NOT SURE. HE'S NOT SURE EITHER.
POOR PETE.
OH, PLEASE. THIS WHOLE THING COULD BE OVER IN LIKE TEN SECONDS. WITHOUT A SINGLE INJURY.
BECAUSE THE KID RIGHT IN FRONT OF US IS SPIDER-MAN.

THE PREVIOUS DAY.
I'M EMMA FROST.
THIS IS MY FRIEND, SOPHIA SANDUVAL, BETTER KNOWN AS CHAT.
WE'RE TOP MODELS AND NEED TO TAKE THESE DRESSES FOR A PHOTO SHOOT. IT'S AN HONOR FOR YOU. SAY YES NOW.
YES.
SORRY!
HI. I'M EMMA. THIS IS SOPHIA. WE'RE SPECIAL OPERATIVES FOR THE FBI. WE NEED TO REQUISITION YOUR MEALS.
SURE.
NO PROBLEM.
SORRY!
MY FRIEND'S NAME IS SOPHIA, BUT MOST PEOPLE CALL HER CHAT.
CHAT? WAIT. LET ME GUESS. IT'S BECAUSE YOU CHAT ONLINE A LOT?
SOMETHING LIKE THAT.
UMM, THERE'S LIKE, BIRDS ON YOUR SHOULDERS.
BIRDS.
SOMETIMES YOU'RE KIND OF EMBARRASSING.
I CAN'T HELP IT!
ANIMALS SENSE THAT I CAN UNDERSTAND WHAT THEY SAY, AND THEY'RE SOOO EXCITED TO TALK WITH ME!
IT'S LIKE WHEN YOU'RE IN A FOREIGN COUNTRY, AND YOU DON'T KNOW THE LANGUAGE, AND THEN YOU FIND SOMEONE WHO DOES SPEAK ENGLISH, AND YOU CAN'T STOP TALKING TO THEM!

BESIDES, I EMBARRASS YOU?
YOU'RE THE ONE TAKING OVER PEOPLE'S MINDS, LIKE MAKING THIS CABBIE DELIVER ALL OF THIS STUFF BACK HOME.
I DON'T TAKE OVER ANY MINDS. I JUST SUGGEST THINGS TO PEOPLE.

I'VE BEEN THINKING ABOUT GOING BACK TO SCHOOL.
I KNOW.
IF I DO, WOULD YOU COME WITH ME?

SO WHAT DO SQUIRRELS TALK ABOUT?
FOOD. IT'S ALWAYS FOOD. THAT'S ALL THE ANIMALS EVER WANT TO TALK ABOUT.
BORING. AND PRIMITIVE. YOU WANT ANY CHOCOLATE?
YES, PLEASE.

THAT'S NOT REALLY ME ANYMORE. IF I--

LOOK OUT!
UMMPP!!
OOOPHH!

KRR-CHASSSHH

ARE YOU OKAY?
Y-YES, BUT... THE SIGN FELL?
WE WERE JUST UNDER IT.
HOW DID...
HOW DID YOU MOVE SO FAST?

IS THAT WORKER WEBBED TO THE WALL?
UMM, YES.
SPIDER-MAN WAS HERE. DIDN'T YOU SEE HIM?

NO.
SPIDER-MAN? THAT WEIRD GUY?

DON'T MIND CHAT. SPIDERS CREEP HER OUT. THEY SAY VILE THINGS.
MY NAME IS EMMA FROST.
I'M PETER PARKER.
LOOK, IF THE TWO OF YOU ARE OKAY, I NEED TO, UHH, GO SOMEPLACE.

WAS SPIDER-MAN REALLY AROUND? DID YOU SEE HIM?
I BET I COULD ASK THE BIRDS. THEY WOULD--
SHUSH.

WAIT FOR IT.

OH MY GOSH! SPIDER-MAN!
PETER WAS RIGHT!

PETER *IS* SPIDER-MAN.
WHAT?

WHEN HE *TOUCHED* ME, I ACCIDENTALLY *FLASHED* INTO HIS *MIND.*

THE *IMPRESSIONS* WERE *SO STRONG!* HIS MIND IS LIKE... LIKE THIS *ENORMOUS BONFIRE!*
BUT HE'S JUST A *LITTLE* GUY. A *REGULAR* KID.

A KID WHOSE *MIND* I WAS JUST *INSIDE.* I *KNOW* WHAT I SAW.
HE *SENSED* THE FALLING SIGN, SOMEHOW.
SPITZ PIZZA

SPRAYED HIS *WEBBING* FROM A *METAL WRISTBAND. SAVED* THAT *WORKER.*

A WRISTBAND? YOU MEAN HIS WEBBING ISN'T NATURAL?
NO, IT'S NOT.
I SUPPOSE THAT'S GOOD. LESS CREEPY, FOR SURE.

NATE'S
I NEED TO GET TO KNOW HIM.
YOU THINK HE'S CUTE?
NO, YOU'RE THE ONE WHO THINKS HE'S CUTE.
AHHH! QUIT READING MY MIND!

DO YOU THINK HE'S A MUTANT? LIKE WE ARE?
HARD TO TELL. HIS MIND IS COMPLEX. HE'S REALLY SMART FOR ONE THING. AND HIS EMOTIONS ARE ALL OVER THE PLACE.

HE LOOKED SO YOUNG. WHY WOULDN'T HE BE SPIDER-BOY?
MAYBE HE'S COMPENSATING FOR SOMETHING?
ANYWAY, I'M... I'M PRETTY SURE IT WAS HIM. MINDS ARE REALLY DIFFICULT TO READ SOMETIMES.

HE'S PROBABLY JUST SOME GUY WITH A SPIDER-MAN FIXATION, SEEING FANTASY VISIONS IN HIS OWN HEAD.
EMMA, LET'S JUST LET THIS DROP, OKAY?

NO WAY. KNOWING SPIDER-MAN'S IDENTITY IS VALUABLE. WE HAVE TO PURSUE THIS, FIND OUT THE TRUTH.
WE CAN USE THIS. HAVE SOME FUN.
USE THIS? THAT SOUNDS WRONG. PEOPLE HAVE A RIGHT TO PRIVACY.
WHATEVER. PRIVACY IS FOR PEOPLE WHO CAN'T READ MINDS. I HAVE TO DO WHAT'S BEST FOR ME.
C'MON! I JUST NEED TO GET A LITTLE CLOSER. HE'S JUST BARELY OUT OF MY MENTAL RANGE.
NO. EMMA! NO!
CLOSER. CLOSER. AND... CONTACT! THERE.
THERE WHAT?
STORE
I KNOW WHERE HE GOES TO SCHOOL.

MONDAY MORNING: 11:22 A.M.
SO THE VIRUS WAS GENETICALLY ENGINEERED TO ATTRACT PHOSPHATES?
EXACTLY. AND ITS BEHAVIOR WAS ALTERED SO THAT IT NATURALLY ATTACHES ITSELF TO CARBON NANOTUBES.

THEN, WE'RE TALKING ABOUT A VIRUS THAT IS, IN EFFECT, A MICROSCOPIC BATTERY.
EXACTLY. THE POTENTIAL FOR MICROELECTRONICS IS UNLIMITED. RESEARCHERS AT STARK INDUSTRIES COULD--
IT SEEMS TO ME THAT THE POTENTIAL FOR GREAT HARM IS THERE AS WELL.
IT IS. BUT WHEN KNOWLEDGE IS THERE TO BE FOUND, IT'S THE RESPONSIBILITY OF THE GOOD GUYS TO FIND IT FIRST. KNOWING IS HALF THE BATTLE...
BUT IF THE KNOWLEDGE IS HIDDEN IN THE FIRST PLACE, THEN--
KNOWLEDGE NEVER STAYS HIDDEN. THERE'S ALWAYS SOMEONE WHO UNCOVERS IT. THAT MAKES IT OUR DUTY TO--

THAPPTT
PETER PARKER, PLEASE REPORT TO THE PRINCIPAL'S OFFICE.

HAVE TO GO!

AHH, PETER. COME IN.
SORRY ABOUT THE ABRUPT SUMMONS, BUT WE HAVE DISTINGUISHED VISITORS.

THIS IS EMMA FROST, VISITING US FROM HARVARD.
MS. FROST IS A RESEARCH PSYCHIATRIST, WORKING ON A GRANT ABOUT SCHOLASTIC PRESSURES ON TEENAGERS. SHE REQUESTED YOU AS A TEST SUBJECT.
CHAT? ARE YOU LISTENING?
SHE... DID?
THIS IS EMMA.

I'M ESTABLISHING OUR MENTAL LINK. DON'T WORRY...PETER WON'T KNOW WE'RE IN HIS MIND.
AND I'M SOPHIA SANDUVAL. JUST CALL ME CHAT.
I'M ANOTHER ONE OF EMMA'S GUINEA PIGS.
BY THE WAY, HE REALLY DOES THINK YOU'RE ADORABLE.

DON'T I KNOW YOU TWO FROM SOME-WHERE?
UHHH, NO?
DON'T WORRY ABOUT THIS EITHER.
WE HAVE NEVER MET.
I'M BLOCKING HIS MEMORIES OF US FROM YESTERDAY. IT'S AS EASY AS IT WAS TO CONVINCE THE PRINCIPAL THAT I'M FROM HARVARD.

I'LL LEAVE YOU TO IT, THEN. CALL IF YOU NEED ANYTHING. I COULD HAVE SANDWICHES SENT IN. SOME SODAS? ANY-THING?
GOURMET PIZZAS, PLEASE, FROM LE SAUCE OLYMPUS. IT'S MY FAVORITE PIZZERIA. DRIVE THERE YOURSELF.
OF COURSE.
SORRY!
NOW THEN, TELL ME A LITTLE ABOUT YOUR LIFE.
NOT MUCH TO TELL. I'M YOUR AVERAGE HIGH SCHOOL STUDENT. MAYBE A LITTLE BIT MORE INTO MATH, THE SCIENCES.
YOU LIKE SCIENCE?
CHAT? CAN YOU SEE THIS?
I'M SENDING YOU MENTAL IMAGES. THIS IS WHAT PETER THINKS OF WHEN HE'S THINKING ABOUT SCIENCE.
HE THINKS ABOUT BEING BITTEN BY A SPIDER?
OH...RIGHT. YOU CAN'T HEAR HIS MIND THE WAY I CAN.
THE SPIDER IS RADIOACTIVE. I THINK THIS IS HOW HE GOT HIS POWERS. SO, HE'S NOT A MUTANT LIKE WE ARE...
BUT HE IS SPIDER-MAN. PETER PARKER IS SPIDER-MAN.
NEVER GOT MUCH INTO SPORTS, REALLY. I'M NOT THE ATHLETIC TYPE...

I WISH YOU COULD SEE MORE THAN JUST THE IMAGES. HE'S SO POWERFUL!
HIS CONFIDENCE IS AMAZING...AT LEAST WHEN HE'S IN COSTUME.
MAYBE THAT'S WHY HE CALLS HIMSELF SPIDER-MAN.
I LIVE ALONE WITH MY AUNT MAY...
WHAT HAVE WE HERE? THERE'S A BLOCK IN HIS MIND.
EMMA...WE SHOULD LEAVE IT ALONE. IF HE DOESN'T WANT TO--
I'M GOING DEEPER. HMM... THERE'S SOMETHING HERE ABOUT A BURGLAR.
A BURGLAR? WHAT DO YOU MEAN? HE STOPPED A BURGLAR?
NO, HE DIDN'T. HE LET HIM GET AWAY.
DON'T SEE WHY IT'S SUCH A BIG THING. IT'S NOT LIKE IT WAS HIS RESPONSIBILITY TO--
OH. OH NO.
WHAT? WHAT IS THIS WE'RE SEEING?

THIS IS HOW HIS UNCLE BEN *DIED.* AND THE *BURGLAR* THAT PETER, THAT *SPIDER-MAN,* LET GO FREE...
...*HE'S* THE ON WHO *DID* IT.
OH PETER. I'M *SO* SORRY.
HMM? FOR *WHAT?* MY GRADES ARE *GOOD,* AND I SHOULD BE ABLE TO GET A *FULL SCHOLAR-SHIP* INTO--
NEVER MIND.
SO...UMM... CHANGE OF SUBJECT. ARE THERE ANY *GIRLS* IN YOUR LIFE?
CHAT!
I'M JUST *ASKING.* IT'S *RESEARCH.*
I REALLY DON'T HAVE MUCH *TIME* FOR A *SOCIAL LIFE* THESE DAYS.

WELL, I CAN SEE *WHY* HE DOESN'T HAVE MUCH FREE TIME.
BUT WHY DOES HE *FIGHT* THESE GUYS? I DON'T SEE WHAT'S *IN IT* FOR *HIM.*

OH EMMA. CAN'T YOU SEE?
HMMM? SEE WHAT?
HE BLAMES HIMSELF. WITH THE POWERS HE HAS...THE WAY HE LOST HIS UNCLE BEN... HE FEELS THAT HE CAN'T LET ANYONE ELSE GO THROUGH THAT TRAGEDY.
HE FEELS THAT WITH HIS GREAT POWERS COMES A GREAT SENSE OF RESPONSIBILITY.
CHAT...HOW ARE YOU READING THIS? YOU SHOULDN'T BE GETTING ANYTHING BUT VISUALS.
BUT IT'S SO BRIGHT! HOW CAN I NOT SEE IT? HE'S SO...SO--
NOBLE.
HUH?
WELL, I THINK THAT'S ABOUT ENOUGH FOR TODAY.
IT'S POSSIBLE THAT I MIGHT WANT TO DO SOME FOLLOW-UP QUESTIONS AT SOME TIME.
OH? UHH, SURE.

AND PETER, YOUR PRINCIPAL SHOULD BE BACK WITH THE PIZZAS SOON, COULD YOU BE A DEAR AND MEET HIM IN THE MAIN HALL?
UMM, I GUESS. BUT I SHOULD BE GETTING TO--
THANKS! CHAT AND I HAVE AN APPOINTMENT TO KEEP.
WE DO?
MMM-HMMM. A LITTLE SOMETHING I SET UP EARLIER. A CHANCE TO SEE THE SPIDER-MAN IN ACTION.
EMMA, WHAT ARE YOU PLANNING?
YOU'LL SEE.
HMM, LOOK, THERE'S A NEW GIRL IN SCHOOL.
HOW CAN YOU TELL?
HER THOUGHTS ARE VIVID. SHE'S STRONG-WILLED.
SHE'S NERVOUS ABOUT TRANSFERRING HERE TO A NEW SCHOOL. EXCITED, TOO.
ALSO, I'M READING SOME WORRY OVER HER DAD BEING A POLICE OFFICER.
AHH. HERE WE GO.
MONEY.
MONEY.
MONEY.
MONEY.
MONEY.

QUIT STALLING! I KNOW YOU GOT THE PAYROLL GOLD! HAND IT OVER!
DID YOU SET THIS UP?
HMMM? ME? YOU SUSPECT ME OF PLANTING MENTAL SUGGESTIONS INTO THE MINDS OF FOUR STREET THUGS?
DO I LOOK LIKE THE TYPE OF PERSON WHO MADE THEM BELIEVE THAT THEY ARE STAGE-COACH ROBBERS, TOLD THEM THERE WAS A DELIVERY OF GOLD HERE AT EXACTLY THIS TIME, ALL SO THAT I COULD WATCH PETER PARKER CHANGE INTO SPIDER-MAN AND FIGHT THEM?
GEEZ. YOU'RE JUST... URRGGG!
OKAY. SO WHAT'S PETER THINKING?
RIGHT.
SO, MAYBE MENTALLY "SUGGEST" EVERYONE LOOK THE OTHER WAY FOR A MOMENT?
IN A SECOND. FIRST I WANT TO SEE HOW--
HE DOESN'T KNOW HOW TO CHANGE INTO COSTUME.
YOU MEAN, WITHOUT GIVING AWAY HIS SECRET?

GET OUT OF MY SCHOOL!
WHOA!

PETER'S GONE!
THAT GIRL! SHE WAS ENOUGH OF A DISTRACTION THAT--
UGGH!
THWIP
CHAT! THIS IS EXCITING!
UNNHH!
TRY TO KEEP AN EYE ON WHAT--
HIS SPEED IS--! HE'S--
UNHH!

HE'S SO STRONG!
NO! GET AWAY FROM ME YOU CREEPY--
OH!

WELL, THAT WAS EXCITING.
NOW WHAT? YOU FEEL LIKE CATCHING A PLAY?
I CAN GET US TICKETS FOR ANY OF THE SHOWS JUST BY...
UMM, NO.

EXCUSE ME? NO?
I THINK THIS, THIS SCHOOL...I THINK THIS IS WHERE I SHOULD BE.
OH, YOU'RE BACK ON THAT SCHOOL THING.

I'M NOT BACK ON IT. I'M ALWAYS ON IT.
I NEED SOMEONE IN MY LIFE BESIDES ALL THE SQUIRRELS AND CROWS AND SPARROWS. I NEED SOME FRIENDS WHO--

SO I'M NOT GOOD ENOUGH FOR YOU SUDDENLY?
EMMA, WE'VE SPENT THE LAST TWO DAYS BASICALLY ROBBING FROM PEOPLE! EXCEPT FOR THE PART WHERE WE WERE INVADING THE MIND OF THE MAN WHO SAVED OUR LIVES!
THAT'S NOT WHAT I WANT TO BE ABOUT!

JUST, LET ME DO THIS. I HAVE TO GO TO SCHOOL.
I'LL ALWAYS WANT TO BE YOUR FRIEND, BUT I WANT TO BE SOMETHING ELSE, TOO.

THIS ISN'T ABOUT PETER BEING KIND OF NEAT, IS IT?
HUH? NO! IT'S THAT I--
I WAS KIDDING.
OKAY, CHAT. I'LL BUMP A FEW MINDS AROUND. LET'S GET YOU BACK TO SCHOOL.
REALLY? OH...THANKS. EMMA, I... THANKS!

TUESDAY MORNING.
SO, THIS IS YOUR FIRST DAY?
ENROLLED JUST THIS MORNING.
I'M A LITTLE FLUSTERED, SO THANKS FOR SHOWING ME AROUND.

SURE. IT'S TOUGH BEING THE NEW KID.
BELIEVE ME, I KNOW WHAT IT'S LIKE TO FEEL DIFFERENT.

OH, AND PETER... THANKS FOR LETTING ME BORROW YOUR CHEMISTRY TEXTBOOK.
NO PROBLEM. I SAW YOU LOOKING A BIT LOST IN CLASS, AND I HAD TO DO SOMETHING.

NOBODY ELSE DID ANYTHING TO HELP. MOST PEOPLE THINK IT'S FUNNY IF SOMEONE ELSE IS HAVING TROUBLE.
WELL, NOT ME. MAYBE I HAVE AN OVERDEVELOPED SENSE OF RESPONSIBILITY.

I DON'T THINK SO. I THINK YOU'RE SWEET.
REALLY? THANKS, CHAT.
UMM, I'LL SEE YOU AROUND, OKAY?
I HOPE SO--

SPIDER-MAN.
END

#54

PETER?
PETER PARKER?
HUH?
TAKEN FOR A RIDE
PAUL TOBIN WORDS
MATTEO LOLLI PENCILS
CHRISTIAN VECCHIA INKS
SOTOCOLOR COLORS
DAVE SHARPE LETTERS
SKOTTIE YOUNG COVER
DAMIEN LUCCHESE PRODUCTION NATHAN COSBY EDITOR
JOE QUESADA EDITOR IN CHIEF DAN BUCKLEY PUBLISHER
ALAN FINE EXECUTIVE PRODUCER

IT'S GWEN. GWEN STACY.
REMEMBER? CALCULUS CLASS?
OF COURSE I REMEMBER!
SORRY TO BLURT OUT YOUR NAME, BUT I SAW YOU AND DAD WAS JUST BUGGING ME ABOUT MAKING FRIENDS AT MY NEW SCHOOL--
--SO I THOUGHT, "HEY! THERE'S SOMEBODY I KNOW."
SEE, DAD? LOOK. A FRIEND. I TOTALLY HAVE FRIENDS.
IT'S TRUE. I'VE BEEN WATCHING HER AROUND SCHOOL, AND SHE ALREADY KNOWS MORE PEOPLE THAN I DO.
HMMM. INTERESTING. BEEN WATCHING ME AROUND SCHOOL, HUH?
WHAT? NO! NOT LIKE... THAT.
I REMEMBER GWEN TALKING ABOUT YOU, PETER. SHE SAYS YOU'RE MIDTOWN'S SMARTEST STUDENT.
I'M NOT SURE THAT'S--
IT'S COMPLETELY TRUE. NO DOUBT.
WELL, THAT'S GOOD AND BAD. IT CAN BE LONELY BEING THE SMARTEST GUY AROUND.
DAD'S A POLICE CAPTAIN HIS "SUPERIORS" AREN'T AS SMAR AS--

GWEN... SHUSH.
ANYWAY, PETER, YOU CAN JUST CALL ME GEORGE. I'M NOT A POLICE CAPTAIN RIGHT NOW, AND--

--AND--

OFFICER! WHAT'S GOING ON!
OH, CAPTAIN STACY! ARMED ROBBERY CALL! IN THE PARK! JUST DOWN THE BLOCK!

GWEN! PETER! YOU TWO STAY--
HUH? WHERE DID PETER GO?
HE WAS JUST HERE.

YOU STAY HERE!
I DON'T WANT YOU ANYWHERE NEAR THE TROUBLE!

OH. SURE.
LIKE I LOVE IT WHEN YOU GO FIGHT THE BAD GUYS.

THE SITUATION?
FOUR MEN.
THEY'VE DONE TWO *SMASH'N GRAB ROBBERIES* FROM THE FOOD CARTS.

THERE'S BEEN A *RASH* OF SIMILAR ROBBERIES OVER THE PAST COUPLE WEEKS.
LOOKS LIKE *THESE* ARE *OUR GUYS.*

ARMED?
WITH *BATS.* MAYBE *MORE.*
AND THEY HAVE *HOSTAGES.* HOW DO YOU WANT TO *HANDLE* THIS?
WHO ARE THE HOSTAGES?
A YOUNG BOY AND HIS SISTER.
THEY WERE BUYIN
PRETZELS. GOT
CAUGHT UP IN THI

THWIPP
UH?
WHAT IS THIS?
THWAMPPT
AHH!
WHOA! DANG! SPIDER-MAN!
GET THAT CART!
SPIDER-MAN?
AWESOME!
WELL... THE INTERNET. NEWSPAPERS. THEY'RE FULL OF STORIES ABOUT--
ABOUT SPIDER-MAN BEING A CRIMINAL?
SPIDER-MAN! HE'S IN ON IT!
SHOULD WE TAKE HIM DOWN, CAPTAIN STACY?
TAKE HIM DOWN? WHY?
THE MEDIA IS FULL OF STORIES ABOUT HOW ALL COPS ARE ON THE TAKE, TOO.
DON'T BELIEVE EVERY-THING YOU READ. NOT WHEN YOU'VE GOT EVIDENCE RIGHT IN FRONT OF YOUR EYES.

KEEP OFF
HE GRASS!
HEY GUYS! WHERE YA GOING? DIDN'T YOU SEE THE SIGN?
HERE! TAKE A CLOSE LOOK!
YOU KNOW, EVERY-ONE SHOULD TAKE THE TIME TO READ, BECAUSE...
WHUMMPF
OH, YOU'RE ALL UNCONSCIOUS, HUH?
WELL, I GUESS IT'S LONELY BEIN THE SMARTEST G AROUND.
DID... DID YOU JUST--?

SMARTEST GUY AROUND!
IDIOT!

YOU'VE BEEN SO QUIET ALL NIGHT. EVERYTHING OKAY, PETER?
SURE. FINE, AUNT MAY.

SURE. *FINE*, AUNT MAY.
JUST PRACTICING ON KEEPING MY STUPID MOUTH SHUT.

MIDTOWN HIGH. NEXT MORNING.
FIFTY DOLLARS AND YOU CAN BORROW MY CAR.
FIFTY? CAN'T YOU--
IT'S A DATE. YOU WANT TO TAKE HER ON A BUS?
--TOLD HER THAT HER COAT LOOKED TOO MUCH LIKE MINE AND SHE'D HAVE TO RETURN IT.
--HE WAS TELLING ME ABOUT ALL THESE THINGS HE'S DONE AND I WAS TOTALLY WEIRDING OUT, UNTIL I REALIZED HE WAS TALKING ABOUT SOME ONLINE GAME.

PETER.
SOPHIA! HI! GOOD MORNING!
CALL ME CHAT. ALSO... TWO GREETINGS? DO GIRLS MAKE YOU NERVOUS?
WHA...? I--
SO THE REASON I'M HERE IS BECAUSE I HAVE TO TAKE A WOUNDED RACCOON ON A ROAD TRIP.

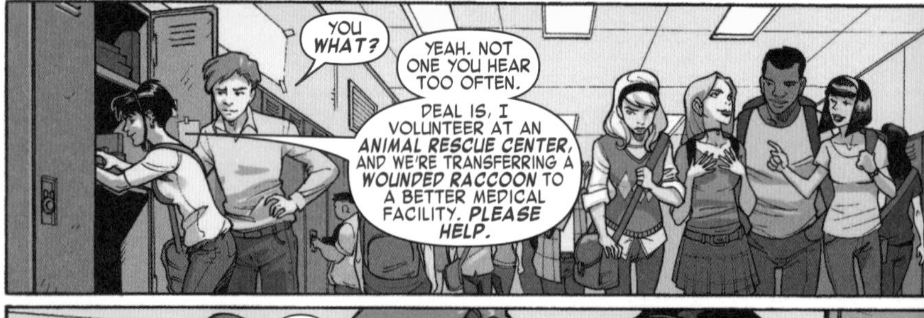
YOU WHAT?
YEAH. NOT ONE YOU HEAR TOO OFTEN.
DEAL IS, I VOLUNTEER AT AN ANIMAL RESCUE CENTER, AND WE'RE TRANSFERRING A WOUNDED RACCOON TO A BETTER MEDICAL FACILITY. PLEASE HELP.

ME?
YES. I WANT YOU TO COME ALONG. WILL YOU? PLEASE SAY YOU WILL. I'M NERVOUS ABOUT THIS.
YOU WOULD TOTALLY BE MY HERO.

I...GUESS I COULD HELP. SURE.
GREAT! YOU'RE DRIVING. YOU HAVE A CAR, RIGHT?

A CAR?
IN EXCHANGE FOR DOING THIS, I WILL TOTALLY LET YOU TAKE ME TO THE THREE STOOGES FESTIVAL AT THE ALADDIN THEATER.
FIVE HOURS OF YOU AND ME AND THE STOOGES. AND POPCORN.

REALLY? I SAW AN ARTICLE ABOUT GIRLS NOT LIKING THE STOOGES.

AND BY THIS YOU'RE SAYING I'M NOT FEMININE? DON'T I LOOK LIKE A GIRL TO YOU?

SO, TOMORROW THEN. AFTER SCHOOL. IT'S A DATE.
PICK ME UP AT THIS ADDRESS. I'LL HAVE A RACCOON WITH ME.

AND TALK MORE TOMORROW, OKAY?

A CAR?

HOW AM I SUPPOSED TO GET A CAR?
AND GOOD JOB WITH THE "GIRLS DON'T LIKE THE STOOGES" COMMENT, PARKER.

ANOTHER QUIET NIGHT, PETER. ARE YOU SURE EVERYTHING'S OKAY?
WHAT?
CARS AND RACCOONS.
NOTHING, AUNT MAY. SORRY.

DID SHE SAY IT WAS A DATE?

AND I TOTALLY TOLD HIM IT WAS A DATE!

YOU DID NOT!
I DID, EMMA! YOU KNOW I CAN'T LIE TO YOU!
WELL, YOU COULD RIGHT NOW, BECAUSE I CAN'T READ MINDS OVER THE PHONE.

TOO BAD. IF YOU LOOKED INTO MY MIND, YOU'D SEE HOW I COMPLETELY BOWLED HIM OVER.
REALLY? WOW. AND TO THINK HE'S SPIDER-MAN.

WELL, HE WAS PETER PARKER, RIGHT THEN.
WHATEVER. SAME DIFFERENCE.

THE IMPORTANT THING IS THAT YOU'RE BEING VERY SNEAKY AND MANIPULATIVE, AND I, EMMA FROST, RESPECT AND COMMEND YOUR EFFORTS.

SNEAKY AND MANIPULATIVE? REALLY? MAYBE PETER SHOULD BE NERVOUS.
BUT I DON'T HONESTLY THINK I'M--
OOH! HAVE TO GO!
DIAMONDS EVERYWHERE! I'LL BRING YOU SOME!

NEXT MORNING.
PETER, YOU'RE SMART, RIGHT? I MEAN, YOU KNOW EVERYTHING.
EVERYTHING? NOT QUITE THAT MUCH, GWEN.
MORE SCIENCE THAN MOST PEOPLE, I SUPPOSE.

BUT I MEAN AROUND SCHOOL. YOU HEAR THINGS, RIGHT? BECAUSE I'VE HEARD THAT CRAIG BONZER AND HIS FRIENDS ARE RENTING OUT THEIR CARS TO OTHER STUDENTS.
I'M TOO YOUNG TO RENT FROM ANY OF THE REGULAR CAR SERVICES.

CRAIG BONZER RENTS CARS?
I NEED TO GO TO A FRIEND'S WEDDING. IT'S AT A CHURCH ABOUT A HUNDRED MILES OUT OF THE CITY AND I WANT TO DRIVE.
CAN'T YOUR DAD DRIVE YOU?

BEING A NEW YORK POLICE CAPTAIN TAKES LIKE, FIFTY HOURS A DAY.
BUT HE COULD RENT A CAR FOR YOU.
HE COULD IF HE THOUGHT I SHOULD GO. HE SAYS IT'S TOO FAR FOR ME TO DRIVE.

HEY, YOUR DAD, DID HE MENTION ANYTHING...ODD ABOUT ME?
NO. WHY? WHAT?
KEEP THE FOCUS, PETE. WE'RE TALKING ABOUT BONZER. THIS CAR RENTAL THING SOUNDS A LITTLE--

SKETCHY?
MAYBE.
OH! THERE'S BONZER.

HI. I'M GWEN. YOU'RE CRAIG BONZER, RIGHT? I HEAR THAT YOU RENT OUT CARS?
I DO. NEED ONE?
TWO, ACTUALLY.

TWO?

TWO CARS? SURE. WE CAN DO THAT. MY FRIENDS AND I ALL HAVE CARS, SO THERE'S NO WAITING.
LET ME MAKE SOME CALLS. SEE WHAT'S AVAILABLE.

TWO CARS?
I NEED ONE, TOO.
I'VE GOT A DATE WITH...
...I MEAN, SOPHIA SANDUVAL AND I ARE TAKING A RACCOON TO AN ANIMAL HOSPITAL.

OH. A RACCOON. AND...SOPHIA SANDUVAL?
THAT'S... NICE.

SHE DIDN'T SEEM SO NERVOUS.

WELL, IF YOU HAD HEARD WHAT SHE WAS--I MEAN, I'M PRETTY GOOD WITH ANIMALS, SO I COULD SENSE SHE WAS NERVOUS.

SPEAKING OF...

ANIMAL SHELTER
ANIMAL SHELTER

EMMA! I'M ON THE DATE RIGHT NOW!
NO. NOT THE STOOGES. THE ANIMAL SHELTER.
YES. I LIKE HIM. YES. HE SEEMS TO LIKE ME.

NO. I'M OUTSIDE. I NEEDED TO GET SOMETHING FROM OUR CAR.
GUESS WHAT? I TOTALLY ALMOST BLURTED OUT THAT I CAN TALK TO ANIMALS!

DO YOU THINK HE WOULD UNDERSTAND? I MEAN, ME BEING A MUTANT AND ALL?
WITH HIM BEING SPIDER-MAN, MAYBE HE'D BE MORE ACCEPTING.
WHAT? NO! OF COURSE I HAVEN'T TOLD HIM THAT WE KNOW!

WEIRD. SOME DUDE IS STARING AT OUR CAR.
NO. HE'S NOT LOOKING AT ME. DEFINITELY THE CAR.
YES. I KNOW I'M PRETTY.

YEAH. I'M SURE IT'S YOUR CAR.
I JUST PICKED UP MY DOG FROM THE VET, AND HERE'S YOUR CAR. RIGHT IN THE PARKING LOT.

STEAL IT BACK? YOU GOT IT, BOSS.

HEY.
HUH?

ANNNHHH!
NOBODY MESSES WITH THE TORINO GANG!

WHUFF WHUFF WHUFF
YOU STOLE THE WRONG CAR, LADY!

DON'T YOU MOVE, LITTLE GIRL! DON'T YOU MOVE AT ALL!
WE GET BACK TO TONY, HE'LL HAVE SOME QUESTIONS FOR YOU.
LIKE, WITH TORINO IN CHARGE OF HALF THE CRIME IN QUEENS, WHY DO YOU THINK IT'S OKAY TO DRIVE OFF WITH ONE OF HIS CARS?
WHUFF
WHUFF
WHUFF

PLEASE! I DON'T KNOW ANYTHING ABOUT--
WHAT YOU NEED TO KNOW IS HOW TO SHUT UP!
AND ANOTHER THING, I--
OH MAN!

PETER!

PETER? WHO'S PETER?
UMM. PETER. IT'S MY DOG. BACK AT THE--
SHUT UP ABOUT YOUR DOG!

I'M OKAY! I'M OKAY! GOTTA KEEP CALM.
HE CAN'T DO MUCH WHEN I'VE GOT THIS CHICK IN THE CAR!
THWUUUUMPP
AHHHH! GEEEZZ!
RARRR RARRR RARRR RARRR RARRR RARRR RARRR
STOP BARKING AT ME! YOUR MASTER IS THE ONE WHO'S BAD!
RUMPH?

OKAY. RIGHT.
LET'S SEE IF HE'S A HERO OR NOT!
WHAT ARE YOU DOING? YOU CAN'T JUST--
HE CAN EITHER STOP ME, OR SAVE THE CROWD!
HAVE A NICE RIDE, SWEETIE!!
THWIP
THWIP

UNNHHH!
STAY BACK! STAY AWAY FROM HIM! HE'S DANGEROUS!
UHH.
SPIDER-MAN! ARE YOU OKAY?
FINE. JUST NEED TO...CATCH MY BREATH. CAN'T LET HIM GET AWAY.
DON'T WORRY. HE'S NOT GETTING FAR.

HE RAN INTO A LITTLE TROUBLE.
WHAT THE...? GET THESE THINGS OFF ME!
WHUFF
WHUFF
WHUFF
WHUFF
WHUFF
WHUFF
THOOKKT
JEEZ, DUDE. YOU HAVE A SUIT MADE OUT OF BREAD-CRUMBS, OR SOME-THING?

SOME FIRST DATE, HUH?
WHAT?

I MEAN... UHH...I WAS ON A DATE!
I NEED TO GET BACK TO THE SHELTER OR HE'LL BE WORRIED!
OH, YEAH. I'VE GOT... SOMEWHERE TO GO, TOO.

THANKS FOR SAVING ME!

NEXT MORNING.
SO CRAIG BONZER AND HIS FRIENDS WERE STEALING CARS?
EXACTLY. DAD TOLD ME ALL ABOUT IT.
APPARENTLY IT STARTED OUT WITH THEM JUST LOANING THEIR OWN CARS, BUT MORE AND MORE FRIENDS WERE ASKING, SO THEY STARTED STEALING CARS TO MEET THE DEMAND.
THEY MAKE A LOT OF MONEY?
WEIRDLY, NO. THE WEREN'T ACTUALL SELLING THE CAR JUST HELPING OU FRIENDS.
I HOPE DAD GOES EASY ON THEM.
ME TOO. BONZER ACTUALLY DID SEEM SORRY. AND A LITTLE SCARED.
HMM? WHEN DID YOU SEE THEM?
UMM, NEVER. I JUST MEANT THAT IN HIS CASE, I'D BE SORRY.
OH.
YOU KNOW SOMETHING NEAT? DAD TOLD ME THAT SPIDER-MAN CONVINCED BONZER AND HIS FRIENDS TO TURN THEMSELVES IN. MOST PEOPLE THINK SPIDER-MAN IS A CRIMINAL, BUT DAD DOESN'T.
ME NEITHER. I THINK HE'S KIND OF AMAZING.
REALLY?
WEIRD, HUH? MAYBE YOU SHOULDN'T TELL ANYONE.
DON'T WORRY, GWEN. I'M REALLY GOOD AT KEEPING SECRETS.
...EN

#55

3:45 P.M. PRINCIPAL TAGGERT'S OFFICE.
MIDTOWN HIGH QUEENS, NY.
THERE'S A REALLY GOOD EXPLANATION FOR WHERE I'VE BEEN.
SO YOU'VE SAID.

BUT AFTER THE TWO OF YOU WERE SEEN LEAVING SCHOOL GROUNDS TOGETHER AT LUNCH-TIME, IT SEEMS TO ME THAT--
WE WEREN'T LEAVING TOGETHER. PETER WAS--
--SIMPLY FOLLOWING YOU. SO YOU SAY.
I WAS FOLLOWING HER. SHE SEEMED SAD AND I WANTED TO KNOW IF SHE WAS OKAY. BUT I LOST HER.
AND APPARENTLY LOST THE SCHOOL AS WELL, SINCE YOU MISSED THE ENTIRE AFTERNOON'S CLASSES.
BEYOND THAT, IF YOU WEREN'T TOGETHER, WHERE WERE YOU? I KEEP HEARING WHAT YOU WEREN'T DOING, BUT I'M NOT HEARING WHAT YOU DID.
ONLY BECAUSE YOU REFUSE TO BELIEVE THAT--
THAT YOU SKIPPED HALF A DAY'S CLASSES BECAUSE OF A FAMILY EMERGENCY INVOLVING THE MAFIA?
MS. STACY... I KNOW THAT YOU'RE NEW, BUT HERE AT MIDTOWN HIGH WE'RE NOT FOND OF SUCH WILD STORIES.
FINE. THEN WAIT FOR MY DAD. HE'LL EXPLAIN THIS.

WE'LL SEE.
NOW THEN, MR. PARKER. YOU SAY YOU WEREN'T WITH GWEN. SO, WHERE ELSE?
I WAS... HELPING A FRIEND.

NOT GOOD ENOUGH.
WHAT FRIEND? AND WHY DID THEY NEED HELP?

WHY I WAS LATE FOR CLASS
PAUL TOBIN STORY
JACOPO CAMAGNI PENCILS
SOTOCOLOR COLORS
DAVE SHARPE LETTERS
SKOTTIE YOUNG COVER
DAMIEN LUCCHESE PRODUCTION
NATHAN COSBY EDITOR
JOE QUESADA EDITOR IN CHIEF
DAN BUCKLEY PUBLISHER
ALAN FINE EXECUTIVE PRODUCER
IT WAS A PERSONAL THING.

8:03 A.M.
BZZZZZZZZZZZZZZZZZZZZZ
FIRST BELL, GWEN. TIME FOR CLASS.
GWEN

GWEN, ARE YOU... CRYING?
I CAN'T TALK RIGHT NOW. OKAY?
IF THERE'S ANYTHING I CAN DO, JUST--

NOT NOW, PETER. PLEASE... JUST. PLEASE.

OKAY. SEE YOU IN CLASS.

HMMM. WHAT WAS THAT ABOUT?
HUH? OH, HI, CHAT.
THAT WAS A MAJOR LEAGUE BLOW-OFF. LOOKED LIKE IT HURT.
SOMETHING'S BOTHERING HER.
THAT WAS GWEN STACY, RIGHT?
YEAH.
8
DID YOU DO SOMETHING TO MAKE HER MAD? IT WASN'T A LOVER'S QUARREL, WAS IT?
DID YOU BREAK INTO HER WEBPAGE AND LEAVE A BUNCH OF WEIRD PHOTOS?
FINALS-
ERLEADER
CONTE
BZZZZZZZZZZZZZZZZZZZ
I'M NOT EVEN SURE SHE HAS A WEB-PAGE.
THERE'S THE SECOND BELL. WE SHOULD GET TO CLASS.
CHEEP CHP CHEEP
YES. THANK YOU. I DID NOTE THAT HE AVOIDED THE "LOVER'S QUARREL" PART OF MY QUESTION, BUT I DON'T THINK IT MEANS ANYTHING.
CHEEP CHP CHEEP
NOW QUIT CHIRPING.

10:30 A.M. ADVANCED CHEMISTRY CLASS.
SOMETHING BOTHERING YOU, PETER? YOU SEEM BARELY BRILLIANT.
SORRY. JUST THINKING OF A FRIEND.

11:30 A.M. STUDY HALL.
PETER. YOU AND ME. LUNCH. I'M PICTURING A SALAD WITH ICE CREAM DRESSING. YOU IN?
FOR LUNCH WITH YOU, I AM IN. FOR ICE CREAM SALAD, I AM OUT. AND CULINARILY DISGUSTED.

STOMACHS NEED ADVENTURE, TOO. SOME NIGHT I'LL LET YOU HAVE A TASTE OF MY OLIVE AND PEANUT BUTTER SHAKE RECIPE.
I TREMBLE WITH HORRIFIED ANTICIPATION.
MEET ME IN TEN MINUTES OUT FRONT, OKAY? I NEED MY PURSE.

FIVE MINUTES LATER.

GWEN?

GWEN! WAIT!

GWEN?
OTOBIN'S TAMALES
JEEZ, SHE'S FAST!
'SCUSE ME. COMING THROUGH.
WHERE THE HECK IS SHE--
--THERE!
AHHH!
WELL, IF IT ISN'T GWEN STACY! WHAT A SURPRISE!

TOMBSTONE!
YEAH. AND GUESS WHAT? I STOLE YOUR DAD'S PHONE AND SENT THE EMERGENCY TEXT, BECAUSE I WANTED TO MEET YOU.
NOW HERE YOU ARE. LET'S COMMEMORATE WITH SOME PICTURES, SHALL WE?
CLICK
CLICK
CLICK
CLICK

C'MON, SMILE! YOU CAN GIVE THESE TO YOUR DAD! HE'LL BE HAPPY TO--
CLICK
CLICK
CLICK
LEAVE MY DAD ALONE!

BAM
YOUR DAD NEEDS TO LEAVE US ALONE.
SO YOU GIVE HIM THESE PICTURES, REMIND HIM HOW MUCH TROUBLE HE'S MAKING, AND HOW MUCH TROUBLE YOU COULD BE IN.

OOOO! CAN I BE IN THE PHOTOS? I LOVE PHOTOGRAPHY! KIND OF A HOBBY OF MINE.
SPIDER-MAN?

DIDN'T EXPECT YOU. PROWLING THE SUBWAYS NOW?
CHEAPER THAN CABS. HOW'S THE MOB THESE DAYS?

WOULDN'T KNOW. NOT ASSOCIATED.
NOT PUBLICLY. NONE OF YOU ARE. SPEAKING OF THAT, YOU FEEL LIKE FIGHTING HERE IN THE SUBWAY?
FIGHTING A SUPER HERO IN THE NEW YORK SUBWAY SYSTEM WHILE TRYING TO ABDUCT A TEENAGE GIRL...THAT SOUNDS LIKE A LOT OF PUBLICITY.
SURE YOU WANT THAT?

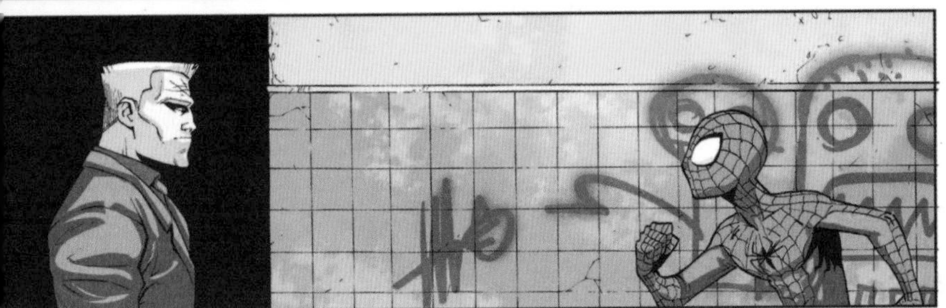

I WASN'T ABDUCTING HER.

AND WHO SAYS YOU'RE A SUPER HERO?

UP CLOSE, YOU'RE SMALLER THAN I THOUGHT YOU'D BE.
OUCH. YEAH. IT'S BECAUSE I KEEP GETTING DEFLATED.

FURYFILES.COM
NO! I MEAN, SORRY! I MEAN, OH MY GOSH THANK YOU SO MUCH! THAT MAN, HE'S CALLED TOMBSTONE. HE'S...
HE'S KNOWN MUSCLE FOR THE MOB. WHAT'S HE WANT WITH YOU?

MY DAD IS CAPTAIN STA-UMM, HE'S A POLICE CAPTAIN. HE'S MADE SOME IMPORTANT ARRESTS LATELY.
MADE SOME ENEMIES, TOO?
PLENTY. AND THEY'RE TRYING TO USE ME TO STOP DAD. THEY KEEP CALLING MY PHONE, WRITING MY E-MAIL, ATTACHING PHOTOS OF ME WALKING AROUND TOWN, GOING TO SCHOOL, SHOPPING.
I ALREADY HAD TO CHANGE SCHOOLS BECAUSE OF ALL THIS. IT'S DRIVING ME A LITTLE INSANE.

UMMM...

CAN I ASK YOU SOME-THING?
SURE.
ARE YOU A HERO OR WHAT? TOMBSTONE DIDN'T SEEM TO THINK SO. LOTS OF PEOPLE CALL YOU A VILLAIN.
LOTS OF PEOPLE CAN BE WRONG.
I KNOW. DAD SEEMS TO TRUST YOU, FOR SOME REASON.

OH. THAT'S... REALLY GOOD TO HEAR.
FOR THE RECORD, I ALWAYS TRY TO DO THE RIGHT THING.
THAT'S EVEN A BETTER ANSWER THAN SAYING YOU'RE A HERO.

YOU'RE GETTING SOME ATTENTION.
COULD BE YOU. PRETTY GIRLS ALWAYS GET A LOT OF ATTENTION.
NOT SO MUCH THAT OFFICERS RADIO IN OUR LOCATIONS. BUT, THANKS.

YOU WANT TO CARRY ME UP TO THE ROOF? TALK THERE?
HUH?

I MEAN, SURE. THAT WOULD HELP, ACTUALLY.
I FEEL WEIRD JUST STANDING ON THE STREET.
SO, WHAT DO YOU THINK I SHOULD DO?
I THINK YOU SHOULD NOT LET GO!
OF COURSE NOT. BUT I MEAN I WANT TO HELP YOU AND YOUR FATHER. HOW DO YOU THINK I SHOULD GO ABOUT IT?
WOW. THAT WAS REALLY STRANGE.
GOING UP THE WALL? YOU GET USED TO IT. A WALL IS JUST ANOTHER SURFACE, AND--
I MEANT IT WAS WEIRD HAVING A SUPER HERO ASK WHAT HE SHOULD DO. I THOUGHT YOU GUYS JUST SORT OF DID YOUR THING WITHOUT ASKING ANYBODY'S OPINION.

WELL, I'M NEW AT THIS. ANY IDEAS?
TALK TO MY DAD. TELL HIM I SENT YOU.
AT THIS TIME OF DAY HE'S USUALLY AT THE BEULAHLAND COFFEE SHOP.

I'D CALL AHEAD, BUT I GOT MAD AND THREW MY PHONE AWAY.
BEULAHLAND? THAT'S NEARBY.
I SHOULD STAY HERE. SOMEBODY NEEDS TO TALK TO THE POLICE. LET THEM KNOW YOU WERE DOING HERO THINGS. NOT VILLAIN THINGS.

AND I'M SORRY I CALLED YOU SHORT. IF IT HELPS, YOU'RE REALLY STRONG!
THANKS!

TEN MINUTES LATER.
GREAT.
"HELLO, CAPTAIN STACY. REMEMBER ME? I'M SPIDER-MAN. I'M WANTED BY THE POLICE."
"HI, GEORGE! IT'S SPIDER-MAN. YOU KNOW, PETER PARKER, WHICH I THINK YOU FIGURED OUT THE OTHER DAY WHEN I WAS STUPID AND SAID--"
GRAHHH! I TOTALLY SHOULD HAVE WAITED. BROUGHT GWEN WITH--
SPIDER-MAN.
WHA...!
GEEZ!

DIDN'T MEAN TO STARTLE YOU.
HOW DID YOU SNEAK UP ON--I MEAN, YOU'RE CAPTAIN AMERICA AND--WHY ARE YOU...?
CATCH YOUR BREATH, SON.
SERIOUSLY. LET'S NOT FIGHT, OKAY? I'M ONE OF THE GOOD GUYS.
FINE. I SPEND TOO MANY DAYS FIGHTING.
AND TO ANSWER YOUR QUESTION, I SAW YOU AND TOMBSTONE IN THE SUBWAY, THEN FOLLOWED YOU HERE.

YOU FOLLOWED ME? YOU MUST BE AS GOOD AS I'VE HEARD.
I'M NOT BAD. IF IT MAKES YOU FEEL BETTER, I'M OUT OF BREATH RIGHT NOW.
THANKS. SO YOU WERE IN THE SUBWAY?

"I'VE HAD TOMBSTONE UNDER OBSERVATION FOR A COUPLE DAYS. HE'S THE MAIN SUSPECT IN A COUPLE OTHER INCIDENTS."

WHAT INCIDENTS?
JUST SOME INCIDENTS.
I SAW WHAT YOU DID FOR CAPTAIN STACY'S DAUGHTER. NICE WORK. AND FAST. GOT THERE EVEN BEFORE I COULD.

ZEEEET
ZEEEET
ZEEEET

STACY JUST GOT A PHONE CALL. HE'S ON THE MOVE.
DO WE TALK WITH HIM, OR FOLLOW HIM?
LET'S FOLLOW FOR NOW. I ALSO FEEL WEIRD JUST STANDING ON THE STREET.
JEEZ. YOU HEARD THAT? WHERE WERE YOU?
IN CIVILIAN GEAR. EASIER TO BLEND IN WHEN I'M JUST STEVE ROGERS.
SOMETIMES I WISH I COULD DO THAT. JUST TAKE OFF THE UNIFORM IN PUBLIC.
IT HAS ITS DOWNSIDE. WHEN EVERYONE KNOWS YOUR IDENTITY, IT CAN FEEL LIKE THE COSTUME NEVER COMES OFF.
THAT'S THE DIFFERENCE BETWEEN BEING A PUBLIC HERO, AND A PRIVATE ONE, LIKE YOU.
SOME-TIMES I THINK I'M DOING IT WRONG.
ME TOO. BUT WE CAN ONLY LIVE LIFE THE WAY WE FEEL IS BEST.
STILL, AT TIMES, YOU CHOOSE THE RIGHT DOOR ONLY TO FIND A LABYRINTH, WITH TEN NEW DOORS BEHIND IT.
TRUE. I FEEL LIKE I SPEND ABOUT HALF MY TIME HIDING MY REAL IDENTITY.
CAPTAIN AMERICA IS MY REAL IDENTITY. NOT THAT WAY FOR YOU?
I WANT TO KEEP MY IDENTITIES SEPARATE, IF POSSIBLE.
HOW'S THAT WORKING OUT?
NOT GOOD. I THINK MAYBE HE KNOWS.
CAPTAIN STACY? I'VE HEARD HE'S A GOOD MAN. TRUST-WORTHY.

I HOPE SO.
LET'S SEE IF THERE'S ANOTHER ENTRANCE.
The CoAST
SALE

LOCKED.
HOW STRONG ARE YOU?
EXIT

SKRRUNNNCH
I'M NOT BAD.

LET'S KEEP IT QUIET FROM HERE ON UNTIL WE KNOW WHAT WE'RE LOOKING AT. MAYBE HE'S JUST MEETING A FRIEND.
FROM HIS BODY LANGUAGE, I'D SAY IT'S NOT A FRIENDLY VISIT.
NICE TO HEAR THAT YOU PAY ATTENTION. THIS IS A TOUGH BUSINESS.

SIXTEEN ARRESTS IN THE PAST TWO WEEKS.
SIXTEEN ARRESTS IS SIXTEEN PROBLEMS.

AND WE DON'T LIKE PROBLEMS. FRANKLY, WE DON'T DEAL WELL WITH THEM.
WE AIN'T THE TYPE THAT TURNS THE OTHER CHEEK.
LEAVE GWEN OUT OF IT.

NOT HOW IT WORKS. YOU'RE MESSING WITH OUR FAMILY, AND THAT MEANS WE MESS WITH YOUR FAMILY.
THAT'S FAIR, RIGHT?

YOU LOST YOUR RIGHT TO PLAY FAIR WHEN YOU BROKE THE LAW!
YOU'RE DOING A POOR JOB OF LISTENING TO WHAT I'M SAYING.
I DIDN'T COME HERE TO LISTEN! I CAME HERE TO ARREST YOU!

TO ARREST ME? YOU CAME HERE TO ARREST ME?

GOOD LUCK WITH THAT.

SKRUNNAPT
UNHHHH!

AHHGGH!
YOU AGAIN?! PERFECT!
AW, I'M NOT QUITE PERFECT!
I CAN NEVER GET MY SHIRTS TO FOLD PROPERLY!

JOKE ALL YOU WANT! I LIKE IT! A LITTLE ENTERTAINMENT DURING A FIGHT MAKES ME HAPPY!
SKRASSSHH
DANG! REALLY? BECAUSE I DON'T LIKE YOU WHEN YOU'RE HAPPY!

HAH!
UNNHH!

SPIDER-MAN! GET OUT OF HERE!
I'M NOT LEAVING YOU ALONE!
I'M NOT ALONE!

OKAY, THEN I'M NOT LEAVING YOU AND CAPTAIN AMERICA ALONE!

THWAAKKT

TABLE FOR TWO!
UNKKFFF!
GAHHHH!

YOU HAVE TO GET OUT OF HERE!
DANG IT! I'M ON YOUR SIDE! YOU CAN TRUST ME!

YOU BOYS SHOULD HAVE DONE YOUR RESEARCH. I'M NOT SOME GARDEN-VARIETY PUNK!
I'M TOMBSTONE!!
FWAAACKT
UNGGHH!

THIS IS WHY I HAVE TO STAY!
YOU CAN'T HANDLE TOMBSTONE!

LIKE YOU CAN?!
WHOA!
KEE-RASHHHH

ARE YOU...?
I'M FINE! GO HELP CAPTAIN STACY! I GOT THIS!

YOU GOT THIS?
UNNGHHH!
YOU THINK YOU CAN TAKE ME ON?! I'M TOMBSTONE!
STOP SAYING YOUR NAME SO MUCH!

URRRRR!
WEBBING? YOU THINK THESE TINY STRANDS CAN HOLD TOMBSTONE?
I CAN BREAK FREE OF THIS EASILY!
COULDN'T DO IT, HUH?
I GUESS THAT'S BECAUSE SOMETIMES TINY THINGS ARE REALLY STRONG!
LIKE ME!
NGHHHH!
AND FOR MY SECOND TRICK!

SPIDER-MAN, PLEASE. GO NOW.
SERIOUSLY... QUIT TRYING TO GET RID OF ME! I DON'T SMELL AND I'M HOUSE-TRAINED AND I--
I'VE BEEN TRYING TO TELL YOU I DIDN'T COME HERE ALONE. YOU THINK I'M DUMB?

TOMBSTONE MESSED WITH MY DAUGHTER, AND THAT MEANS HE MESSED WITH THE DAUGHTER OF THE NYPD. IN A FEW SECONDS ABOUT THIRTY COPS ARE COMING THROUGH THAT DOOR.
NOW, I HAPPEN TO THINK YOU'RE ONE OF THE GOOD GUYS.

BUT MOST OTHER COPS THINK YOU'RE A CRIMINAL, AND IF YOU'RE STILL AROUND WHEN THEY GET HERE...
YEAH. MESSY. I GOT IT NOW. I'LL GET WHEN THE GETTING'S GOOD.

WAIT!
YEAH?
ONLY SECONDS TO TALK, SO ANSWER THIS AS QUICKLY AS POSSIBLE. CAN MY DAUGHTER BORROW YOUR MATH HOMEWORK?

HUH? GWEN? WHY?
SHE'S REALLY SMART WITH--

--OH.

I THOUGHT SO.
NOW GET OUT OF HERE! HURRY!

3:55 P.M. PRINCIPAL TAGGERT'S OFFICE. MIDTOWN HIGH.
THANK YOU FOR COMING IN AND CLEARING THIS UP, CAPTAIN STACY.
YOU SAY THERE ACTUALLY WAS A FAMILY EMERGENCY, AND GWEN WAS NEEDED?
THAT'S THE TRUTH. SORRY FOR THE INCON-VENIENCE.

WELL, THAT COVERS MS. STACY'S ABSENCE, BUT I'M AFRAID YOUR ABSENCE REMAINS UNEXPLAINED, PETER.
YOU LEFT WITH, EXCUSE ME, LEFT SHORTLY AFTER MS. STACY. WERE YOU INVOLVED IN THE FAMILY EMERGENCY? WAS GWEN THE FRIEND YOU SAY YOU WERE HELPING?

NO, I WAS--
WAS PETER WITH YOU BY ANY CHANCE, CAPTAIN STACY? ANY LIGHT YOU CAN SHED ON THIS MYSTERY?

SORRY, BUT I HAVE NO IDEA WHERE PETER WAS THIS AFTERNOON.

IT'S A COMPLETE MYSTERY TO ME.
...END

#56

PORT AUTHORITY BUILDING. NEW YORK CITY.
VIGILANTES
PAUL TOBIN WORDS MATTEO LOLLI PENCILS
CHRISTIAN VECCHIA INKS SOTOCOLOR COLORS
DAVE SHARPE LETTERS SKOTTIE YOUNG COVER
PAUL ACERIOS PRODUCTION MICHAEL HORWITZ ASST. EDITOR
NATHAN COSBY EDITOR JOE QUESADA EDITOR IN CHIEF
DAN BUCKLEY PUBLISHER ALAN FINE EXECUTIVE PRODUCER
FIRST, I'M CAPTAIN GEORGE STACY.
SECOND, THANKS FOR YOUR PATIENCE.
THIRD... WHO CAN TELL ME WHAT WENT ON HERE?
TAXIS ONLY
ONE WAY
TAXI
NO WAR
LICE LINE DO NOT CROS

I SAW IT ALL. THOSE GUYS IN THE SUITS WERE TALKING TO SOME BOYS.
YEAH...THEY MUST HAVE JUST GOT OFF THE BUS. THE BOYS, I MEAN.
COULD YOU HEAR WHAT THEY WERE SAYING?
NO SIR. NOT A WORD. BUT THE BOYS SEEMED NERVOUS.
THEY CAME OUT OF NOWHERE!
WHO CAME OUT OF NOWHERE?
THE GUY WITH THE CAPE. AND THE WOMAN.
AHH, DANG. CAPE.
THE WOMAN WAS THROWING BEAMS OF LIGHT AT THE MEN. LIKE THEY WERE DAGGERS. AND THE BIG GUY WITH THE ROBES WAS EVERYWHERE! DIDN'T SEEM REAL.
CLOAK AND DAGGER?
SOUNDS LIKE IT.

TAXI

DID YOU SAY THEIR NAMES WERE *CLOAK* AND *DAGGER?*
THAT'S RIGHT. THE MAN HAS SOME SORT OF SHADOW POWER. THE WOMAN'S LIGHT-DAGGERS DRAIN THEIR VICTIM'S VITALITY, LEAVING THEM EXHAUSTED, HELPLESS.
THEY DON'T SEEM TO BE DANGEROUS, OTHERWISE.
MAYBE.
POLICE

WHAT WERE CLOAK AND DAGGER *DOING?*
NOT SURE. POSSIBLY PROTECTING THE BOYS. THESE ARE *TORINO'S* MEN. A CRIME FAMILY WITH A NASTY HABIT OF *FORCIBLY* RECRUITING MEMBERS TO THEIR GANG.
POLICE LINE
LINE - DO NOT

DID YOU SEE WHERE THE BOYS WENT?
RAN OFF *THAT* WAY. THEY WAS SOME *FAST* KIDS!
AND CLOAK AND DAGGER JUST PLAIN, UHH, DISAPPEARED. LIKE...*POOF!*

LEAVING US WITH NOTHING BUT *THESE* GUYS.
CAPTAIN...WE AIN'T CUT OUT FOR THE *CAPES.* HOW YOU WANT TO *HANDLE* THIS?

LET ME SEE IF I CAN THINK OF SOMETHING.

ELSEWHERE.
CHAT, WHERE DO YOU GET YOUR, UMMM, CULINARY IDEAS?
I MEAN, I'M NOT SAYING A LOAF OF BREAD STUFFED FULL OF ALMOND AND OLIVES AND CHEESE IS A BAD IDEA...
NO...YOU'RE JUST IMPLYING THAT.
EAT IT. YOU'LL LOVE IT. TRUST ME. I'M TOTALLY THE QUEEN OF PICNICS.
I THOUGHT YOU'D BE COMPLETELY INTO TRYING NEW THINGS.
YOU DID? WHY?

BECAUSE YOU'RE, UMMM... I JUST THOUGHT YOU WOULD. THAT'S ALL.
THIS ROOFTOP IS REALLY NICE.
I COULDN'T BELIEVE IT WHEN YOU FIRST BROUGHT ME UP HERE.

MY FRIEND EMMA CONVINCED MY...OUR LANDLORD TO HAVE IT DONE. SHE'S REALLY PERSUASIVE.
IT'S BEAUTIFUL. AND IT SURE ATTRACTS THE ANIMALS.
I CAN'T BELIEVE HOW FRIENDLY THEY ARE. DO YOU FEED THEM OR SOMETHING?

OH, YEAH. I MEAN, SOMETIMES.
IT'S... ACTUALLY, THE THING IS...I'M REALLY GOOD WITH ANIMALS.
YOU MAKE IT SOUND LIKE A BAD THING.

NO! IT'S NOT! I JUST DON'T WANT YOU TO THINK I'M WEIRD OR SOMETHING.
BECAUSE ANIMALS LIKE YOU?

IT'S... UH. NEVER MIND.
PUT SOME HUMMUS ON THAT BEFORE YOU EAT IT.
HUMMUS?

A SPREAD MADE FROM CHICKPEAS, WITH TAHINI, GARLIC, OLIVE OIL, SALT, LEMON JUICE AND SALT. CONSIDER IT A YUMMIER TYPE OF MUSTARD. I MAKE IT MYSELF.
I HAVEN'T EVEN COMPLETELY MASTERED KETCHUP.
REALLY? LOT OF TROUBLE THERE?

LIKE YOU WOULDN'T BELIEVE.
HEY... WHOA! THIS IS REALLY GOOD. I MEAN...THIS IS REALLY GOOD.

I KNEW YOU'D LIKE IT. MY MOM TAUGHT ME HOW TO MAKE THEM. SHE SAID THAT--

OH.

SOMETHING WRONG?
I HAVEN'T TALKED TO ANYONE ABOUT MY MOM FOR A COUPLE YEARS. IT JUST SORT OF SLID OUT.

SEEMS A BIT DANGEROUS HERE, YOU KNOW. SO CLOSE TO THE EDGE.
YOU SERIOUS?

YEAH. OF COURSE.
BUT... WITH YOU...

PETER? CAN I BE REALLY HONEST WITH YOU?
I GUESS SO. ABOUT WHAT?
SECRETS.
WHAT SECRETS?

THAT FIRST DAY WE MET.
AT SCHOOL?
NO. BEFORE THAT. I--
BRINNNGGG

OH GEEZ. I'M SORRY. MY PHONE.

HI. YES. IT'S ME. WHO... UHH.
WHY ARE YOU--?

I NEED SPIDER-MAN.
POLICE LINE - DO NOT
UHH? THIS... OH GEEZ. THIS ISN'T A GOOD TIME.
CLOAK AND DAGGER ARE IN TOWN.
MY MEN CAN'T HANDLE THIS SORT OF THING. I NEED YOU TO FIND CLOAK AND DAGGER. SEE WHAT THEY'RE DOING. WHY THEY'RE IN TOWN.
DON'T ENGAGE THEM. I DON'T WANT YOU GETTING HURT AND I'M NOT SURE IF THEY'RE BAD GUYS ANYWAY. THEY'RE LIKE SPIDER-MAN IN THAT RESPECT. BUT...YOU OWE ME, PETER. AND I NEED YOUR HELP.
IS THIS AN OFFICIAL REQUEST? I MEAN, DO YOUR BOSSES KNOW YOU'RE DOING THIS?
ABSOLUTELY NOT. I CAN'T HELP YOU DO THIS.
BUT YOU CAN FORCE ME TO DO IT.
I'M...NOT FORCING YOU TO DO IT.
WELL...IT SURE FEELS LIKE IT FROM MY END.
I'LL SEE WHAT I CAN FIND OUT.

I HAVE TO GO. I'M REALLY SORRY ABOUT IT AND THE PICNIC WAS AWESOME AND THE STUFFED BREAD THINGY WAS INCREDIBLE AND...
PETER. IT'S OKAY. I'M COOL. YOU OBVIOUSLY HAVE TO DO SOMETHING IMPORTANT. DON'T WORRY. IT'S FINE.
THANKS. I'LL MAKE IT UP TO YOU SOMEHOW.
YES. YOU WILL.
AND...CUE SPIDER-MAN THEME SONG...
NOW.
POLICE

CHECK CASHING

VRRRT

I'M CALLING IT OFF.
OKAY. WHY?
WHAT I DID WAS WRONG. YOU'RE A GOOD MAN. I BELIEVE THAT. AND I WAS USING YOU AND THAT'S WRONG. I'D NEVER FORGIVE MYSELF IF SOMETHING HAPPENED.
YOU'RE THE SAME AGE AS MY DAUGHTER. YOU'RE HER FRIEND. I DON'T KNOW WHAT I WAS THINKING.
IF I HAD AN EXCUSE, I'D SAY IT HAD SOMETHING TO DO WITH TRYING TO RUN A NORMAL GROUP OF OFFICERS, DAY AFTER DAY, OFTEN AGAINST PEOPLE IN CAPES.
IT'S DIFFICULT AND IT'S DRAINING AND I SAW A CHANCE TO USE YOU.
I SHOULD HAVE
COOL.
BUT, YOU KNOW...I'M NOT A PUSHOVER, AND IF YOU DO NEED HELP, YOU CAN CALL ME.
BUT LAY OFF THE IMPLIED THREATS. JUST ASK.
DEAL.

P.S. I'M NOT A DETECTIVE.
I HAVE NO IDEA HOW TO FIND THESE CLOAK AND DAGGER GUYS.

I EVEN HAD TO SNEAK A LOOK AT SOMEONE'S LAPTOP TO FIND OUT WHAT THEY LOOK LIKE.

STILL HUNGRY. WONDER IF CHAT...?

BEING A SUPER HERO SHOULD NOT MAKE ME LEAVE IN THE MIDDLE OF A DATE.

SO, YOU WANT TO GUESS WHAT HAPPENED ON MY DATE WITH PETER?
HMMM... WHAT? UMMM, NO. THAT'S MORE YOUR STYLE, EMMA.
ACTUALLY, I ALMOST TOLD HIM HOW I KNOW HE'S SPIDER-MAN. YES. I DID.

IT JUST SEEMED LIKE THE MOMENT WAS RIGHT, AND HE'S REALLY NICE AND I'M REALLY LYING TO HIM BY PRETENDING THAT I DON'T KNOW, AND THAT MAKES ME FEEL BAD.
YOU CAN'T BE SERIOUS! HIDING SECRETS IS LIKE THE BEST THING EVER!
IT GIVES YOU CONTROL.

BUT I DON'T WANT TO CONTROL PETER. HE'S NOT THAT...I MEAN I'M NOT LIKE THAT.
I EVEN ALMOST TOLD HIM THAT I CAN TALK WITH ANIMALS. HE WOULDN'T THINK I'M A FREAK. I KNOW HE WOULDN'T. HE'S SPIDER-MAN. HE'D UNDERSTAND WHAT IT'S LIKE TO BE DIFFERENT.

NOBODY UNDERSTANDS WHAT IT'S LIKE TO BE DIFFERENT. THAT'S WHAT BEING DIFFERENT IS ALL ABOUT.
WE'RE ALL DIFFERENT IN OUR OWN LITTLE WAYS.

I STARTED TO TALK ABOUT MY MOM.
YOU DID NOT!
I DID. IT SLIPPED OUT.
SOPHIA SANDUVAL, I AM COMING TO SEE YOU. YOU'RE OBVIOUSLY COMPLETELY INSANE FOR THIS BOY!
I THOUGHT HE WAS INTERESTING WHEN I MET HIM, YOU KNOW, WHAT WITH BEING SPIDER-MAN AND ALL, BUT HE'S APPARENTLY EVEN MORE DREAMY THAN I THOUGHT!
I CAN LITERALLY FEEL YOU BLUSHING OVER THE PHONE!

NO, YOU LITERALLY CAN NOT. BUT I WAS BLUSHING, AND IT WOULD BE NICE IF YOU CAME FOR A VISIT. DANGEROUS, THOUGH.
YEP. EXACTLY. DANGEROUS BECAUSE YOU WOULD READ MY MIND, AND IT HAS SOME STRANGE STUFF IN THERE, OF LATE.
REALLY? AND HERE I THOUGHT YOU WERE SUPPOSED TO BE THE INNOCENT ONE.
GUESS THAT'S UP TO ME, NOW. I'LL HAVE TO START WEARING MORE WHITE.
FASHION
SO, DID HE KISS YOU GOODBYE?
NO. HE GOT A CALL FROM THE POLICE, AND THEY'RE BLACK-MAILING HIM INTO FINDING SOME BAD GUYS.
I TOTALLY HAD SOME PIGEONS LISTEN IN ON THE CALL, AND THEY TOLD ME ALL ABOUT IT.
YOU KNOW ANYTHING ABOUT SOME PEOPLE CALLED CLOAK AND DAGGER?

SURE. I'VE STUDIED THEM. I THOUGHT THEY WERE MUTANTS, AT FIRST. BUT THEIR POWERS COME FROM WHEN THEY WERE FORCED INTO SOME SORT OF UNDERWORLD EXPERIMENTS.
NASTY STUFF. THEY'RE LUCKY TO BE ALIVE.
DAGGER'S BOLTS OF LIGHT ARE LIKE ENERGY VAMPIRES OR SOMETHING. THEY STEAL YOUR VITALITY.
CLOAK USES SOME SORT OF DARKNESS, MAYBE EVEN A SHADOW DIMENSION. NOBODY SEEMS TO KNOW.
THING IS, HE CAN USE IT TO TELEPORT AND HE CAN TURN INTANGIBLE AND MAYBE SOME OTHER THINGS. I'VE HEARD THE TWO OF THEM WERE RUNAWAYS, AND I KNOW THEY HAVE SOME SORT OF ONGOING FEUD WITH THE MOBSTERS WHO KIDNAPPED THEM.
DID YOU SAY SHADOW DIMENSION? I MEAN, HONESTLY, DID I JUST HEAR SHADOW DIMENSION?
YOU DID.
WELL THAT FREAKS ME OUT.
NOW I'M REALLY NERVOUS ABOUT PETER GOING AFTER THEM.

TWO BLOCKS AWAY...
BLEH. I SMELL LIKE CITY SWEAT.
NOT THE GOOD PART OF THE CITY, EITHER. I SMELL LIKE ARMPIT CITY SWEAT.

HEY.

HEY.

HEY!
CLOAK! IT'S SPIDER-MAN!

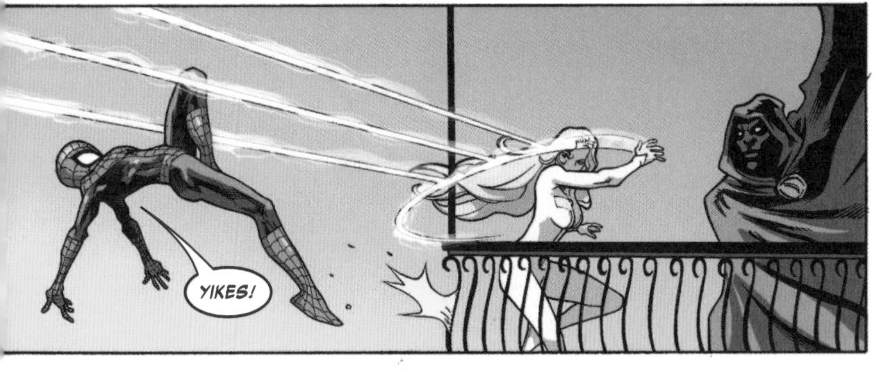
YIKES!

UNHH!
YOU TWO HAVE ONE SECOND TO EXPLAIN WHY YOU'RE STALKING CH-- THAT GIRL!
BECAUSE THAT IS WHAT WE DO. WE SAVE RUNAWAYS.
RUNAWAYS?
YES. A RUNAWAY. WE HAVE COUNTLES ACQUAINTANCES A ORPHANAGES.
SOPHIA... CHAT...USED TO TRAVEL TO ALL TH ORPHANAGES IN TH STATE, HELPING TO RUN A TRAVELLING ZOO.
IT WAS GOOD FOR THE CHILDREN. THEY LEARNED ABOUT RESPONSIBILITY, TAKING CARE OF THE ANIMALS.
A WEEK HERE. A WEEK THERE. SHE WAS SO GOOD WITH THE ANIMALS.
BUT THEN SHE DISAPPEARED! SHE LOVED THOSE KIDS! LOVED THOSE ANIMALS!
SHE WOULDN'T HAVE RUN AWAY! NOT WILLINGLY!

THAT MEANS SOME-ONE TOOK HER!
WAS IT YOU?
ME?
I'VE READ HOW YOU HAVE A LOT OF MOB CONTACTS! IT JUST MAKES SENSE THAT--
WAIT-WAIT-WAIT! ME? MOB CONTACTS?
THE ONLY CONTACT I HAVE WITH THE MOB IS WHEN I'M PUNCHING THEM!

WELL... SOMETIMES I KICK THEM! OR HIT THEM WITH LARGE THINGS!
BUT WAIT! SHE HAD A TRAVELLING ZOO? SHE'S A RUNAWAY?

HOW DOES-- AGGHH!

THAT HAS HIM! HE WON'T BE ABLE TO--

UHHH!
WHAT DID YOU HIT ME WITH? I FEEL... WEAK.
LIKE I COULD BARELY DROP A CAR ON YOU IF YOU KEEP MAKING ME MAD!
I'M IMPRESSED! YOUR VITALITY MUST BE INCREDIBLE!
BUT A FEW MORE OF--
THOKK
UNNHH!
OWWW! WHY DID YOU DO THAT? I'M RESCUING YOU!
NO YOU AREN'T!